EAGLE SONG

ISBN 0-439-09914-5

Text copyright © 1997 by Joseph Bruchac. Pictures copyright © 1997 by Dan Andreasen. All rights reserved. Published by Scholastic Inc., 555 Broadway, New York, NY 10012, by arrangement with Dial Books for Young Readers, a division of Penguin Putnam Inc.
SCHOLASTIC and associated logos are trademarks and/or registered trademarks of Scholastic Inc.

30 29 28 27 26 25   16 17 18 19/0

Printed in the U.S.A.   23

First Scholastic printing, September 1999

Designed by Karen Robbins

Special thanks to my friend Richard Hill, Tuscarora artist, museum educator, and former ironworker from a family of Iroquois ironworkers. Our conversations over the years and his book, Skywalkers: A History of Indian Ironworkers (Woodland Cultural Centre, Brantford, Ontario, 1987), helped me greatly in the writing of this story.

For the Hills
and all those who dream of eagles
while they walk the high iron

EAGLE SONG

▸ JOSEPH BRUCHAC ◂

pictures by DAN ANDREASEN

SCHOLASTIC INC.

New York   Toronto   London   Auckland   Sydney
Mexico City   New Delhi   Hong Kong

▸ 1 ◂

She':kon

"Hey, Chief, going home to your teepee?"

Danny Bigtree clenched his fists but kept walking. The November wind was cold against his face. It blew his long black hair over his eyes. He thought again of cutting it short.

If he asked his mother to cut his hair, she might look at him in that way she had. She wouldn't tell him no, though. Even though her eyes might question his decision, he knew she would cut it if he asked. But he knew, too, that even with short hair he'd still be noticed. The other boys would still say things like that. That's how it always was here in Brooklyn. Especially if you were different.

It would do no good to say, as he had once said to them back in September, "I'm not a chief. We're Iroquois and we never lived in teepees. We lived in longhouses a long time ago, and now I live in an apartment building." They'd just laugh again. Then Tyrone and Brad would ask him where his war pony was.

None of the boys followed him. They went back to their basketball game. Danny stopped at the corner and looked back to watch them play. He wasn't really interested in basketball, but the way they played it almost looked like fun. Some of them were really good, especially Tyrone. While Danny watched, Tyrone bounced the ball, cut around two of the other boys, jumped up and threw the ball in a high long arc. It swished down through the basket.

Brad, Tyrone's best friend, came over and the two boys slapped their palms together in a high five. Danny sighed. He'd never played much basketball on the reservation. Lacrosse was his game. But nobody here played lacrosse.

Danny found himself thinking again of what it had been like up at Akwesasne. The wide St. Lawrence River.

He knew it was so polluted from the factories on the Canadian side that no one could fish in it anymore, but in his memory it was beautiful. Akwesasne. Fields and woods to play in. Lots of other Indian kids who looked and talked the way he did. Akwesasne. The name was so much better than "Brooklyn." Akwesasne meant "The Place Where the Partridge Drums." He didn't know what Brooklyn meant.

There had been plenty of reasons to leave Akwesasne, though. No jobs was one. It was because of the lack of employment that men like his dad traveled all over the country to do ironwork. When his mom had finished her social work degree and been offered the job at the American Indian Community House in Manhattan, she hadn't hesitated. It would be a better life, she'd promised. So far, for Danny, it hadn't been.

He went down into the subway entrance, and when he was on the train, he closed his eyes. That way he wouldn't know if anyone was looking at him. If he kept his eyes closed long enough, he could imagine himself riding on the back of an eagle that would take him away from Brooklyn. It would take him away from schools and tenements and people who made fun of him because he wasn't the same as them. It would take him to a place where there were other people like him and his parents, a far-away place. If he closed his eyes long enough, the roar of the rumbling wheels would become the sound of the waters of the St. Lawrence River going over the stones, the squeaking of the metal of the car would become the songs of birds.

But he couldn't keep his eyes closed too long. If he fell asleep, he might go right by his stop again the way he did last week. Then he wouldn't be able to get home before his mother. She would go to Mrs. Fisher's apartment to pick him up, and he wouldn't be there. His mother wouldn't say anything to him if he came home late, but he'd be able to tell from the look in her eyes that she had been worried.

She already worried enough about Dad and the dangerous work he did every day, fifty stories or more above the earth. Danny didn't want to add to her worries. So he let the sounds of the birds and the clear river flow away from him. Two stops before his station he opened his eyes, and when the familiar letters that spelled out the name of their neighborhood came into view, he stood up in front of the door and got out onto the platform.

When he came out of the subway station, he kept his eyes down on the sidewalk, not looking up at the windows. He could imagine people looking at him from those windows, pointing and laughing.

Danny reached his building. He put his hand down the neck of his sweatshirt and found the beaded string on which the door key hung. At the top of the stairs, he put up his fist to knock at Mrs. Fisher's door.

Their neighbor, a retired lady, gave Danny a snack and kept an eye on him till his mom came home. Salli Bigtree worked until five every day at the American Indian Community House. It sometimes took her an hour to get home from there by subway. Danny usually did his homework and then watched TV with Mrs. Fisher while he waited for her.

But down the hall the door to his own apartment swung open. He saw two things that brought a smile to his face. The first was his mother—home from work much earlier than usual. She had opened the door for him and a very big smile was on *her* face. The second thing Danny saw as he hurried through the doorway was the hard hat placed on the table just inside the door. Painted on the steelworker's cap was a wide-winged eagle sitting on top of a big pine tree.

"Dad is home!" Danny said.

"In the shower," his mother said. "His crew got done on that building in Boston early. He came to the Community House to surprise me. Rosemary told me to take the rest of the day off. I was all through writing my proposal anyway." Danny's mother cocked her head as she looked at him. "You are grinning like a raccoon," she said.

"So are you," said Danny.

"So am I," said his mother. Then she leaned over and hugged him so hard that his feet came off the ground.

Danny hugged her too, and let her lift him up. His mother was very strong. She was almost six feet tall, taller than his father. He thought about how his father always teased his mother about her strength, teased her in a way that made her feel good, even though she would pretend to ignore him.

"Careful there, you're going to break his ribs," boomed a voice as deep and familiar as the beat of a drum.

Richard Bigtree came out of the bathroom, still drying his own long hair. That hair was as crow-black as Danny's except for the places it was flecked with white on his temples. Danny's father was bare-chested and built like a bear. His body was as strong and as round as the trunk of a big pine tree.

Danny's mother dropped him, and Danny ran over to hug his father.

"*She':kon,*" his dad said, speaking the Mohawk word of greeting, the word for peace.

"*She':kon,*" Danny answered, a little catch in his voice as he said it.

"You know why Iroquois men always listen to the women, Son?" his dad said, his arm around Danny.

"No, Dad, why?" Danny said, going along with the joke.

"It isn't just that they are usually wiser than the men," his dad said. Then he paused again. Danny's turn.

"It isn't, Dad?"

"And it isn't just that the women own the households and choose the chiefs."

"It isn't, Dad?"

"No. You know what it is, Dancing Eagle, my son?"

Danny almost laughed then. Whenever his dad talked that way, his face deadpan, his voice imitating a Hollywood Indian, it was time for the punch line. Danny knew what to say next.

"No, my father, what is it?"

"We Iroquois men always listen to the women because if we don't, they will beat us up! Look out, here comes one now!"

Danny's mother grabbed his dad, pushed him back onto the floor, and began to tickle him.

"Help me, my son," his dad cried in a high, funny voice.

Danny jumped in to help. Somehow it ended up with both his mother and his father tickling him. Then, when he had laughed so much it started to hurt, the three of them just stayed there on the floor, their arms around each other.

It's so much fun when Dad is here, Danny thought. Mom doesn't seem so tired when she comes home after work. Why can't it be like this all the time?

But he knew his father's job would take him away again, for weeks and weeks. He knew, too, that he would be back in school tomorrow. Back in that school where no one else was like him, where he had no friends and no one noticed him except to make fun of him.

▶ 2 ◀
Gustoweh

As he did his homework on the small dining room table, Danny listened to his mother and father talking in the kitchen.

"You'll only be home for the week?" his mother's voice said.

"Crew's going to Pittsburgh," his father's voice answered. "It's the Mohawk warrior tradition, Sal. You know, we men go out hunting while the women stay home and take care of the really important things."

"I don't feel like being teased tonight, Rick."

His mother's voice had become serious. Danny realized

how much noise his pencil was making as he scratched it across the paper. He stopped writing and listened harder. But now he could no longer understand what his parents were saying. They were talking in Indian. He had never learned enough Mohawk to understand more than a word or two when people who were really fluent in the language were talking it fast. Even back in the Akwesasne Mohawk School where he used to go, people mostly talked English, except in the Native Culture class. His parents had always intended to send him to a school where Mohawk was spoken a lot of the time—like the Freedom School up on the rez. But then they'd moved to Brooklyn.

As Danny listened closely, though, he heard words that he understood. One of them was his name. His mother said it first and then his father said it, as if he was catching on to something. They didn't say much more in Mohawk, only a few sentences. Then there was a silence.

"Danny," his mother called to him, "clear off the table now so we can set it for dinner."

As the three of them sat together at the dining room table, Danny noticed again how broad his father was. Richard Bigtree looked as solid as a building.

"Will I ever be as big as you, Dad?" he said.

"I'm Wolf Clan," Richard Bigtree said. "We tend to be big people. But you might be bigger. Your mother is Bear Clan and so that's what you are."

"Why don't I belong to your clan?" Danny said. He knew the answer, but he wanted his father to keep talking. It made him feel good to hear his father's voice. Their apartment seemed so empty without it.

"Clan membership always comes from the mother. That is the way it always is among our Iroquois people. It goes back a long time that way. The women are the ones who hold our nations together. We have to remember that." Richard Bigtree looked across the room at his wife. "And if we don't remember it, the women make sure to remind us of it!" Danny's mother made a fist and shook it at her husband as he pretended to be afraid. Danny laughed.

When the dinner was over, Danny and his father went into the kitchen to do the dishes. Danny's mother had to go out to a meeting at the American Indian Community House.

"Try not to wreck the place while I'm gone," she called

from the door, and both Danny and his father rattled the pans as loudly as they could in response.

When they were done, they went into the living room. Danny's father sat in the big chair and picked up the remote control. "What'll it be?" he said. "News or outer space?" He looked down at Danny.

"Dad," Danny said, "can I put on your hard hat?"

Richard Bigtree put down the remote control. "Okay," he said. "But you be careful not to break it. That hard hat is real fragile!"

"You're teasing me, Dad. Didn't you tell me a steel beam could fall on your hard hat and it wouldn't even scratch it?"

"That's right, Son," Danny's father said. "Matter of fact, that's why I'm built like this. Used to be six foot five and skinny as a stick till a steel beam fell on my head while I was wearing that hard hat. Saved my life, but I got squooshed right down so I look like this now. Now I'm five foot nine." Danny's father patted his broad stomach. "And I'm about five foot nine tall too."

Danny laughed. His father pointed with his chin toward the hall and Danny ran to get the hat. He put it on and walked back into the room. He could barely see out from under it.

"In the old days our traditional caps, our *gustowehs,* had three hawk feathers on them, just like those I painted above the eagle on that hard hat you're wearing. That hard hat is what our *gustowehs* look like today, Son," his father said. "That is the cap of a real Iroquois man!"

Danny reached up and took the cap off his head. He ran his palm over the beautiful design of the eagle that his father had painted on the front of the cap. The eagle's wings were spread open wide.

"That eagle there," his father said, "takes care of me. It won't let me fall when I'm up there on the iron."

Danny sat again at his father's feet and put the cap down. "Dad," he said, "I think I need an eagle to take care of me."

His father said nothing. He waited for Danny to continue.

"It's the kids at school," Danny said. "They don't like me. They make fun of me and call me a chief and a redskin and they ask me where my headdress is and tell me to go home to my teepee. I want to kill them. Especially

Tyrone and Brad. They're really good at basketball, but they hate me. Nobody here plays lacrosse."

Danny paused, not sure what he wanted to say next.

"Do the other boys hit you or threaten you?"

"No, at least not yet. But when they're not making fun of me, they just ignore me. Everybody does that, the boys and the girls too. Nobody sits with me at lunch, and in class they only talk to me because we have to talk in our work groups. Dad, I've been here over two months and I don't have one friend. It's like being in a war. And everybody else is on the other side. I don't belong here. I wish we could go back home."

"Your mother tells me," his father said, "that you sit in this chair when I am not here. I guess that is one of the things you and I have in common. Would you like to come over here?"

Danny put the hard hat back on his head and leaned against his father's chair.

"It is hard in fourth grade," his father said. "I remember back when I was in fourth grade. I had a teacher who would beat me. Does your teacher beat you?"

Danny shook his head. For some reason he couldn't say

anything now, and his eyes were wet. He took the hard hat *gustoweh* off his head and rubbed his eyes with the knuckles of his hand. His father began to gently pat his back.

"That's good that your teacher doesn't beat you. You know, when I met her at that open house in September, she asked me to come into your school some time and talk about our form of government. About the way we Iroquois did things. Some of the schools say now that our way of governing ourselves was a model for the American Constitution. So I was thinking about doing that this week, coming in to your class. But I wouldn't want to come to your class if your teacher is one who beats you."

"No, Ms. Mobry is nice. She's awesome. It's the other boys. They might call you names, Dad."

"They might. They might listen too."

Danny's father was silent for a moment and then he took his hard hat and put it on his knee. He began to tap his fingers on the top of the hat in a two-beat rhythm that sounded to Danny like a waterdrum being played for a social dance. His father cleared his throat and then spoke again.

"Son," he said, "I know it is hard to live in a strange place, to be away from home. It's hard to be among people who don't know you. But you aren't the first person who's ever been lonely and without friends. Let me tell you a story, one of the great stories of our people. It might give you strength. It's about the man we call Aionwahta."

"Hiawatha, Dad?"

"Yes, Hiawatha. Not the one in that poem by that man Longfellow, the one you said they had in one of the books in the library at school. This is the real story. You want to hear this story?"

"*Henh!*" Danny closed his eyes as he spoke that Mohawk word his mother had told him was to be said when one wanted to hear a story. When his father's voice spoke the old stories, he could imagine himself in a great bark lodge. He could smell the smoke from the fires, see the snow piled white and clean about the pine trees. The river flowed for him as his father spoke, and he felt at peace.

▸ 3 ◂

The Great Peace

This is the story that Danny's father told:

It was long ago. It was a time when our people had forgotten the original instructions of our Creator. Be good to each other, our Creator told us. Live together in peace. But we had forgotten.

Now our people fought with each other. The Mohawk and the Onondaga, the Cayuga and the Seneca and the Oneida were always at war. It was nation against nation, and within our nations it was village against village. And if one man was killed, then the other men of his village would seek revenge in a blood feud, taking a life for a life.

"The sun itself loves to see war," our people said. "That is why we have such power." And they continued to fight with each other.

Now, among our people there was one man who wanted peace. His name was Aionwahta. He was a Mohawk, but he left the Mohawk people when his sister died. He mourned her death, but the Mohawk people were so used to war and death that they made fun of him in his grief. So he took his canoe and went to the west, toward the lands of the Onondaga.

"I will comfort others who are filled with sorrow," he said, "because no one will comfort me."

Aionwahta had a family, a wife and seven daughers. He worried about what things would be like for his children's children. So while he lived among the Onondagas, he spoke of peace. But the Onondagas were ruled by a man who was a sort of a monster. His name was Adodarhonh and his mind was full of evil thoughts. His thoughts were so twisted that he had snakes growing from his head. His body was twisted too, so that he was crooked seven places in his body, and he had killed many people with his wizardry. He was so evil that he could make birds fall dead out of the sky.

Aionwahta was a great speaker. When he spoke about peace, the people of the warring Onondaga towns came to the council held in his house and listened to him. His words were good.

"Now," the people said, "we must do something about Adodarhonh. We must pacify him, for he continues to kill people. We cannot have peace as long as his mind is not straight."

"This is true," Aionwahta said. "I shall go to Adodarhonh and tell him about peace."

Adodarhonh lived in a nest made of reeds in the swamp on the other side of the lake. "We shall do this," Aionwahta said: "We shall go by canoe across the lake."

But as soon as the canoes were in the lake, the loud voice of Adodarhonh was heard across the waters. "A storm is coming to wash over you!" And as those words were spoken, a great wind came and the waves rose and the canoes were turned over. Many people drowned and the others swam back to the shore.

Once again the people tried to reach Adodarhonh to

bring peace to him. "We shall walk around the lake to come to Adodarhonh's place," Aionwahta said. But as they walked around the lake, the loud voice spoke again, and the ground became marshy and the people could go no farther.

Each time they tried to reach the monster Adodarhonh, they failed. Then a terrible thing happened. One by one, Aionwahta's daughters died—by the evil magic of Adodarhonh.

Now Aionwahta was filled with grief. He did not know how to rid himself of his sorrow. He left the lands of the Onondaga and began to wander. First he went south, up Onondaga Creek. He crossed over Bear Mountain and camped at its foot. That night he heard a song.

Haii, haii Agwah wi-yoh
Haii, haii Agwah wi-yoh

So the song began. *Haii, haii, it is good indeed. Haii, haii, it is good indeed.* Its words were words of peace, and he put that song in his heart and held it.

The next morning he climbed the mountain. There he

saw a wonderful sight. A corn plant was growing there on the mountaintop. It had four roots and five stalks, and on each stalk were three ears of corn. A great turtle with a red and yellow belly was dancing there near the corn plant, dancing the dance which we now call The Great Feather Dance.

"I heard singing last night," Aionwahta said.

"I was the one who sang," said the turtle. "This is the great corn. You will make the nations of the Longhouse like this. The five nations will grow from one plant, and the four roots will stretch to the north and the west, the south and the east."

Then Aionwahta put what he had seen and heard into his heart, and he continued on his way till he came to a group of lakes on a hill. There on the lake closest to him were so many ducks and geese that the surface of the lake could not be seen.

"Why are so many of you here?" Aionwahta said to the birds. At the sound of his voice they all flew up at once and carried with them all of the water from the lake. Then Aionwahta walked across the dry lake bed, where there were many small shells. As he walked among them, he thought of his grief, and he began to pick up the shells and place them in the deerskin pouch that he carried with him. When he had gathered many shells, he continued on his way for two more days, until he came to an old abandoned cornfield and a shelter roofed with cornstalks. He made a campfire there.

Then from the fibers of dried plants he made string, and on the string he placed the shells. When he had made three strings of shells, he put two poles in the ground and laid another pole across them. Then he hung the three strings of shells on the pole and sat there and began to talk to himself. He talked about his grief and how it might be lifted. He bowed his head and talked about peace.

Now, as Aionwahta had traveled from place to place, he had heard of a man who was among the Mohawk people. This man, it was said, was a messenger from the Creator. People called him the Peacemaker.

His coming had been foretold in a great dream which had been sent by the Creator to all of the leaders. In that dream they were told that the word of peace would be brought to them by a man who was a holy messenger. But even though the Peacemaker carried a great message, people were not listening to him. He was not a good speaker because he had been born with a double row of teeth. So when he spoke, his words did not come out clearly.

As Aionwahta spoke to himself the words of peace, he began to understand. One man alone could not bring peace. It had to be done by people working together.

"I must find the Peacemaker," Aionwahta said, and he turned toward the lands of the Mohawk people. Each night he camped and made a fire and hung the three strands of shells from a pole. Each night as he sat, he spoke of peace and said these words: "If I should see someone in grief, I would lift these shells from this pole and console him. The shells would become words, and the darkness would be lifted from him."

At last the smoke from his fire was seen by the chief man of another village. A messenger was sent. When the messenger returned and told of what he had seen—a man sitting by a fire, speaking of peace and the way to lift grief—the head man understood.

"This is Aionwahta, who has left his home at

Onondaga. We have heard of him. He is the one who will meet the great man, the Peacemaker. This, too, was foretold by the dream."

So the head man sent a messenger, and Aionwahta was brought to the village. There he stayed until word came to them about where the Peacemaker was waiting. They traveled many days and when they came to the Peacemaker, the great man rose to his feet and said to Aionwahta, "Younger brother, I see that you are suffering."

Although the Peacemaker's words were not clearly spoken, Aionwahta understood them. He told the Peacemaker of his grief. The Peacemaker listened to his words and took the strings of white shells that symbolized Aionwahta's many troubles.

"Now, younger brother," he said, "I shall lift your sorrow from you."

So it was that the first condolence was done and the first wampum strings were used by our people.

The Peacemaker and Aionwahta formed the plan for a Great League of Peace. The nations which had been at war would join together. They worked together for five years establishing the Great League. Then they returned together to Onondaga. Adodarhonh, who had done all he could to work against this league, knew they were coming. He hid himself so that no one could find him.

But among the Onondagas were two men who could transform themselves into animals. One of them became a bear and the other became a deer, and they went into the forest to seek Adodarhonh. When they came back, they said, "We have found Adodarhonh. He is terrible to see. His body has seven great bends in it and his hair is filled with snakes."

Then the Peacemaker and Aionwahta went with a great multitude of people to the place where Adodarhonh was hiding. As they went, they sang the Peace Hymn which Aionwahta had taught the people, the song given him by the Great Turtle. Their powerful song pierced the air like the cry of the eagle. And they came at last, singing the Peace Hymn, to Adodarhonh's lodge.

Haii, haii Agwah wi-yoh
Haii, haii Agwah wi-yoh

They sang to heal the mind of Adodarhonh, and when he heard the Hymn of Peace, he could not move.

Then the Peacemaker and Aionwahta entered Adodarhonh's lodge. The Peacemaker held out his hand and straightened Adodarhonh's body. Aionwahta combed the snakes from his hair. With his body and his mind healed, Adodarhonh stood and joined them.

Together they dug a hole in the earth and threw the weapons of war into it. Then they planted a pine tree there. The four roots of the pine stretched to the north and the west, the south and the east, just like the roots of the corn plant that Aionwahta saw. That tree stood for their League of Peace. Its roots were white, like the path of peace, and it was said that anyone could trace those roots back to the pine tree and sit under its branches in peace. On top of the pine tree they put an eagle, to keep watch and see if anyone was going to threaten the peace.

In its claws that eagle held five arrows, which stood for the five nations of our people. Alone, you can break one arrow easily. But when you tie five arrows together, it is hard to break them. That is the way we would be. United we would be strong. Together we would work for peace.

So the Great League of Peace was formed by our Iroquois people long ago.

Richard Bigtree paused. "You know what happened to Adodarhonh?"

Danny opened his eyes, almost surprised to see their apartment around them. "No," he answered.

"They set him up as the head of their Great League. To this day his name is passed down to the Onondaga chief who is chosen to head the great council meetings. You see, Son, we believe that a bad human being can be made into a good human being. They can even become leaders, so they can use their energy to do good instead of bad. That is our way."

Danny thought of Tyrone and Brad. "You going to tell that story to my class?"

"Think I should?"

"I like that story. I think they need to hear it in my school."

"I think so too," Richard Bigtree said, running his fingers along the wings of the eagle of peace painted on his hard hat.

▶ 4 ◀

The Visit

Ms. Mobry was writing on the board. She was talking as she wrote, but Danny couldn't hear her words. His heart was pounding so hard in his ears that he couldn't hear anything. It was like having his head under an invisible waterfall, a waterfall as loud as that one up near Saranac Lake where his father had taken him last summer. He looked up at the clock. Wasn't it ever going to be two P.M.?

Danny shook his head and tried to focus on what Ms. Mobry was doing. He watched her hands move. They fluttered like birds as she wrote with the chalk and gestured. Then the buzzer on the intercom sounded. Danny heard that. He almost jumped up to answer it himself.

Ms. Mobry walked over to the intercom. He had never known she could walk so slowly. She pressed the button and Danny saw her lips shape the words. "Yes, what is it?"

As soon as she spoke those words, the invisible waterfall stopped flowing over his head. Danny could hear again. The usual garble of sounds that no one but teachers could understand came out of the intercom grille. Ms. Mobry nodded. She looked over at Danny with a smile and nodded again.

"We have a special afternoon guest," she said to the class. "You can put your math away. We'll have our quiz tomorrow." Twenty-four heads looked up with relief.

"Yes," Danny whispered to himself, "perfect timing, Dad."

"Two people will have to go to the office to escort our guest to the classroom."

Ms. Mobry looked around the classroom at the raised

hands of volunteers sprouting up like small trees. Danny waited for her to call his name.

"Consuela and Tyrone."

Tyrone raised one eyebrow and then lowered it as his name was called. The other kids in the class laughed. Tyrone could always make them laugh. He raised his arms in triumph and started down the aisle. As he brushed by Danny's desk, Danny put his arms over his books. Maybe it had been an accident, but that morning as he walked by Danny's desk, Tyrone had knocked everything onto the floor with his elbow.

Consuela's desk was on the other side of the classroom. As she walked across toward the door, she did a pirouette. Another ripple of laughter ran through the classroom and Ms. Mobry joined in. Everybody knew Consuela was a dancer. That made her popular. She was nice to people too. Danny had to admit that. He was glad that Consuela was going to escort his father to the classroom. But Tyrone? That could be a disaster. What if Tyrone made fun of his father?

The classroom door closed and Ms. Mobry was talking again.

"We haven't begun our unit on Native nations yet. So before our guest comes, let me tell you a few things about the Iroquois." Ms. Mobry wrote IROQUOIS on the board. Then she told the class how the Iroquois call themselves the People of the Longhouse.

"They were a confederacy of Native nations living in the area we now call New York State," she said. "They were good farmers and hunters and great warriors when they defended their homes and their families." Danny knew all of that, but he smiled at what Ms. Mobry said next.

"The Iroquois lived in long buildings called longhouses, not teepees," she said. Then she looked straight at Danny. "Because I want you all to know that Native American people are not just part of the past, I have invited our special guest to come to class today. He's the father of one of our students. And here he is now!"

Danny looked toward the door. Lately he had been looking at that door a hundred times every day.

He would look at it worrying about what would happen when he went through it to go to gym. Just yesterday as they reached the door, someone had pushed him from behind and he'd hit his elbow so hard on the doorjamb that he had to struggle to hold back the tears. He would stare at the doorway, thinking about how he'd be able to get through without bumping into Tyrone or Brad on his way to lunch. He had been looking at it waiting for the final bell so he could go through that door and go home.

This time, though, his father was standing in that dangerous doorway. It was so strange to see his father there with Consuela and Tyrone that Danny almost laughed. But he didn't.

Consuela was smiling and looking up at Danny's father. Danny knew that his father had probably said something funny. She was carrying the big leather bag that Danny's father always kept behind his chair in their living room.

Tyrone was carrying something too. It was Richard Bigtree's hard hat. As Danny watched, Tyrone put the hard hat down carefully on the little table Ms. Mobry had placed at the front of the room.

"Consuela and Tyrone, thank you. You may sit down now," Ms. Mobry said. "Class, this is Mr. Richard Bigtree, Daniel's father. He is a member of the Mohawk

Nation, one of the five nations that make up the Iroquois Confederacy."

Richard Bigtree flashed a smile at his son and then looked out around the class as he took something out of his bag.

"Who knows what this is?"

Danny knew what it was: a wampum belt. His father had made it, copying the design of the ancient Hiawatha Belt. On the belt in purple and white beads were the shapes of a tall tree and four squares, symbols of the founding of the Great League of Peace.

"Is it a headband?" someone said from the back of the room.

Danny's father shook his head.

"Is it a belt?" Consuela said.

"That's good," said Danny's father. "But what kind of belt is it?"

A boy named Kofi raised his hand on the other side of the room. Danny's father nodded to him.

"I know," Kofi said. "It's a wampum belt. I saw one at the museum last week."

"That's right," Danny's father said. "It's a wampum belt. To us it is like a book because it tells a story. Would you like to hear that story?"

"Yes," everyone said.

And Danny listened again as his father told the story of the coming of peace, the story of Aionwahta.

Danny's father finished his story and looked at the classroom. No one moved or said a word. He smiled.

"Has anyone ever seen that pine tree anywhere?"

No one answered him. Then he held up his hard hat, and some of the kids laughed.

"It's on your hat," said a boy in the front row. Danny was surprised. The boy, whose name was Tim, was never the first to answer any question. Tim looked back at Danny and grinned.

Richard Bigtree nodded his head.

"One of the first flags that the United States used had a pine tree on it. The founders of this country, Benjamin Franklin in particular, knew about the Iroquois League. Old Ben Franklin said that the colonists ought to band together like the Iroquois nations did. A lot of people who study how governments are made now think that the United States Constitution is partially modeled after the Iroquois. Any of you got a quarter?"

Everyone in the class began searching their pockets. Danny, though, had been waiting for this moment. He had the quarter ready in his hand.

"Here, Dad," Danny said, tossing the quarter to him.

Richard Bigtree reached out one big hand and caught the quarter without even looking at it. He held it up.

"You see what's on one side of this? It's an eagle, just like the one on my hat. Just like the one on top of that big pine tree. What's it holding?"

Brad raised his hand. "I know," he said. "It's holding thirteen arrows. They stand for the thirteen colonies."

"Just like our Iroquois eagle that holds five arrows standing for the five Iroquois nations."

"Awesome," Brad said.

Tyrone had his hand up now. Richard Bigtree nodded to him.

"What happened to that Adodarhonh dude?" Tyrone said.

"Any ideas?" Richard Bigtree said.

"Maybe they put him on trial and then sent him to the electric chair," said Tyrone. The class laughed.

Richard Bigtree laughed too, but he shook his head. "No, that's not what they did."

"Did they banish him?" Consuela said.

"No." Mr. Bigtree explained what he had told Danny, about how a bad human being could be made into a good one. "If you believe in peace, then an enemy can become a friend," he said.

Tyrone started to raise his hand again, but just then the bell rang. Ms. Mobry stood and held her hands up, palms toward the class.

"Everyone," she said, "tomorrow is Friday and we *will* have that test then. So be prepared. Now, before we leave, let's give Mr. Bigtree a round of applause to thank him for taking the time to share his wonderful story."

The class exploded into applause and Danny's father smiled back at them. He looked at Danny and winked.

Danny winked back. It was great that his father had come to school. But would the kids treat him better now?

▸ 5 ◂

The Longest Day

Although June 21st was supposed to be the longest day of the year, Danny knew that wasn't so. Friday, any Friday when there was school, was really the longest day. Friday always crept by so slowly. It taunted you because you knew that when it was over, it would be the weekend.

This Friday already seemed as if it was going to be even longer than most. Not only was there going to be an afternoon test, it was also the day after his father came to class. Danny had hoped that things would be better today—but so far, things had been worse.

It had started with the phone call last night. The phone had been ringing when the two of them got home from Danny's school. Richard Bigtree had another building project to go to. A microwave tower near Philadelphia. Usually there'd be some downtime between jobs, but this one was a hurry-up deal. The tower was half-done and some of the crew that had been working on it had quit. They'd be working over the weekend, but the pay would be even better than usual. Danny's father had to go because he was the chief of his connecting crew. The connectors were the ones who worked on the very top of the structure being built.

So, early that Friday morning, even before Danny woke up, his father left. He'd go straight from Philadelphia to the Pittsburgh job. He wouldn't be back for two whole weeks!

Danny stayed in bed, not wanting to get up. His mother was in such a bad mood that Danny knew he couldn't talk to her. She banged the dishes in the kitchen sink while she was washing them, and then she dropped something. Danny heard it fall to the floor and shatter. Then everything became quiet.

Danny began to worry about his mother. He padded into the kitchen in his slippers to help her pick up the pieces. But she was just sitting on the floor and crying.

Danny put his arm around her and patted her on the back the way his father always did with him. But it didn't work. It just made her cry harder.

"Mom," Danny finally said, trying to make his voice deep and certain like his father's, "you got to go to work."

"I know," his mom said. "Thank you, Daniel." That worried Danny even more. His mother only called him Daniel when she was upset with him or when she was really, really sad. But she got up off the floor.

As his mother got her things together, Danny came up and stood beside her. "Mom, I'm going to walk you to the station."

"You don't have time. You'll be late to school," his mother said.

"You could give me a note," Danny suggested.

His mom thought about that. "Okay," she said.

Danny stayed close to his mother's side all the way to her subway station, and she hugged him hard before going down the steps. He waited until she was out of sight, then turned and walked the other way to his station.

Danny had never been late for school before and he wasn't quite sure what to do when he arrived and saw the familiar front yard of the school completely empty of kids. It was so quiet! He walked through the front door and nodded to Mr. Kinkaid, the uniformed security guard.

Mr. Kinkaid was cool. He was almost seven feet tall and had been a basketball player. He was from Jamaica and spoke with an accent that Danny really liked. A lot of the kids liked Mr. Kinkaid's way of saying things. You could sometimes hear them imitating the way he said things, especially "man." Mr. Kinkaid said it as if there were several extra letters in the word.

"Mahhnn," Mr. Kinkaid said, looking down at Danny and shaking his head, "you lose your wristwatch?"

Danny shook his head and Mr. Kinkaid smiled. "Through the doorway."

Mr. Kinkaid took Danny's lunch box and looked in it as Danny walked through one of the four metal detectors. Two years ago a fifth grader had brought his father's loaded .38 into the school. Now going through the metal detectors was a part of the routine of every school day.

"You are clean, mahhnn," Mr. Kinkaid said, handing Danny back his lunch box. Danny paused, uncertain what to do.

Mr. Kinkaid bent down. "What's the matter?" he said. "Don't you know what to do when you're late like this?"

Danny shook his head.

"Do you have a note from your mother?"

Danny nodded.

Mr. Kinkaid stood up straight again and smiled. "No problem, mahhnn," he said. "Show the note at the office, then go to your room."

Mrs. Carter, the administrative secretary in the office, took Danny's note without even looking up from her desk. She glanced at it, nodded, and jotted something down on a sheet. Then she reached out to press a button on the console in front of her and spoke into the microphone.

"Ms. Mobry," she said, "Daniel Bigtree. Excused tardy. On his way to class now."

Mrs. Carter looked up at Danny. "Remember the way?" she said.

Danny nodded, but he didn't move. He felt like everything around him was moving in slow motion. It was almost like a dream where your feet are covered with glue
and you can't move them to run or walk.

"Then go to your classroom."

Danny turned and moved his feet, unsticking them from
the floor one step at a time. The hall was long and, except
for the sound of his feet, quiet. He remembered a movie
he had seen on TV. In one scene someone was walking
down a long corridor with many doors in it. The person
walked and walked, and then all of a sudden a monster
jumped out and grabbed him. Danny pictured that monster looking a little like a cross between Tyrone and Adodarhonh in his father's story. The monster would be even
taller than Mr. Kinkaid and it would roar at him as it
jumped out of the doorway.

But Danny made it to the door of his classroom without
a monster getting him. He reached out his hand for the
doorknob and paused. Had his father's visit made a differ-
ence? Or would things be just the way they were before?
When he opened the door, it made one of the loudest
sounds Danny had ever heard. Everyone looked at him as

he closed the door behind himself and stood there. Someone laughed.

"Take your seat, Daniel," Ms. Mobry said. Then she started reading again. Danny liked this book, but today he hardly heard it. He was looking at the clock again, hoping it would magically leap ahead and it would be time for recess. But the clock still moved slowly.

One breath in and one breath out is at least a second, Danny thought. If I breathe in and out sixty times, it'll be a minute.

Tick by tick and breath by breath, the morning crept past. One minute, five minutes, ten minutes. It was endless. Then, somehow, it was time for them to go outside.

Danny walked out into the school yard, trying to act casual. People usually didn't notice him. Why should today be any different? But Consuela was waving at him. He looked around. Maybe there was someone behind him she was waving to? No, there was nobody else. She was smiling, and she motioned for him to come over to the place where she stood with a group of other kids by the swings.

Danny began to walk across the end of the basketball court to reach the swing set.

"Yo, Hiawatha!" someone yelled.

Danny turned to look. It was Tyrone, standing twenty feet away from him.

"Here!" Tyrone shouted. He threw the basketball he had been holding straight at Danny.

Danny tried to get his hands up in time. He couldn't. The basketball came flying at him, getting bigger and bigger until it was all he could see. It hit him square in the face. There was a blinding light and a sharp pain all at once. Danny went down onto one knee and put a hand up to his face over his mouth and nose. One of the fifth-grade teachers, a man whose name Danny wasn't sure of, was coming over to him. Mr. Rosario? Mr. Mario? His nose was aching now and his mouth felt warm and moist. He had to remember the name of the teacher.

As the teacher helped him up, Danny saw Tyrone. He hadn't moved. His mouth was open and he was staring at Danny. Brad grabbed Tyrone's arm and pulled at him. The two boys turned and ran away.

"What happened?" the teacher said. Mr. Rosario. That was his name.

"I . . ." Danny tried to talk, but his mouth was full of

blood. His nose was bleeding too, and it was dripping onto the pavement of the school yard.

"Madre de Dios," Mr. Rosario said. He quickly pulled out some Kleenex tissues and pressed them against Danny's nose.

"I slipped and hit my face on the ground," Danny said. He saw Consuela out of the corner of his eye. She had heard what he said.

"Just hold these tissues tight," Mr. Rosario said. "I'll get you in to the nurse."

By the time Danny reached the nurse's office, a strange thing had begun to happen. The day which had crept along like a snail had started to go faster and faster. Somehow, as he sat there and the nurse took care of him, it became lunchtime. Someone had brought his lunch box.

"You'd better eat," said the nurse. "That was some gusher you had, kiddo! Your nose isn't broken, but you lost a lot of blood. You might feel a little light-headed, so you got to get some food into you, laddie."

Danny ate. The cut on his lip didn't hurt much when he ate. His nose still felt like it was twice as big as his face, though. When he was done, he looked up at the clock. Another hour had gone by. He started to stand up when the nurse came back in, then sat down again, feeling dizzy.

"Whoa there," she said. "You look like you need to take it easy. Let's get you to this cot."

Danny let the nurse lead him to the bed.

"I called your mother," the nurse said as Danny put his head down on the pillow. "Just so there'll be someone to make sure you get home okay. She's leaving work early to pick you up."

Danny closed his eyes. It didn't seem as if he slept, but when he opened his eyes again his mother was sitting next to the cot, holding her purse.

"Are you okay?" His mother's voice, calm but concerned, made him feel better.

"I'm fine. Maybe I ought to go back to class."

"On Monday," his mother said. She looked up at the clock.

Danny looked up at the clock too. School had been out for half an hour! It was past time to go home. Somehow this longest day had become one of the shortest ones.

▶ 6 ◀
Colors

Danny woke up later than he had intended on Saturday. He looked at the digital clock next to his bed. Danny liked that clock because it was green, a color that made him think of home back on the reservation. The green of the grass in the fields. The green of the trees. Even the St. Lawrence River looked green sometimes. Green, green, green 10:16.

10:16! Danny liked to sleep a little late on the weekends, but not this late. Weekend mornings there were TV shows he liked to watch. And most weekends his mother didn't have to work and they could go places together.

There was a park they liked. If they sat very still, the squirrels there would come right up and eat the peanuts that Danny and his mom placed on the ground. Sometimes they would go to the zoo. His favorite place there was the big flight cage with the eagles in it. Danny felt as if those eagles knew him. If he whistled to them, they would look at him and whistle back. Once one of them had flown down and landed on a branch so close to him, he could have reached through the wire and touched it. But he didn't. He knew that eagles were to be treated with respect.

Danny listened. He could hear his mom in the kitchen. She'd call him soon to come and eat. She had to work this weekend. There was a special event at the American Indian Community House. But she was going to take him with her. Other people brought their children, and some of the kids were his own age. It was always easy to play with the other Indian kids. They understood the kind of problems he had in school because a lot of them had similar problems. It wasn't easy being an Indian in the city.

"Danny," his mother called.

"I'm coming, Mom."

Even before the elevator door opened, Danny could hear the sound of kids running on the hardwood floor of the Community House. The door opened and there was Will Tiger leaning against the wall.

"*Yah-tah-hey,* Danno," Will said. *Yah-tah-hey* was a Navajo way of saying hello. Will was Seminole and his family had originally come from Florida. But Will and Danny had heard a Navajo flute player perform at Community House, and now the two boys always greeted each other that way.

"*Yah-tah-hey,*" Danny said.

Will eyed the swelling around Danny's mouth and nose. He didn't ask anything about it. Danny knew that Will wouldn't say anything unless Danny told him about it first. For a moment Danny thought about telling Will how Tyrone had hit him with the basketball. But as he thought that, Danny started wondering. Had Tyrone really meant to hurt him with the basketball or was he just throwing it to him?

Will grabbed him by the arm. "Come on, let's check out the gallery. There's a cool new art show."

Danny followed Will back into the gallery. Will was shorter than Danny, even though he was a year older. He went to a school in the Bronx where gangs were really important. In that school, after you got to fifth grade, just about everyone who was anyone had to belong to one gang or another.

As they walked, Danny noticed the red handkerchief that stuck out of Will's back pocket. The laces on Will's sneakers were red too. Those sneakers were the kind that a famous basketball star always wore. Everyone wanted sneakers like that, but Danny had never seen a pair with red laces. He stopped, staring down at the sneakers.

Will turned to look at him.

"You're in a gang now," Danny said.

"When you're in a gang, it's like a big family," Will said.

"Don't the gangs try to kill each other?" Danny said.

Will looked troubled. "If somebody disses you, you can't just let them do that. You got to be respected to be a man. The gangs are the future, Danny. They're going to be in every school. They're the only way you can survive."

"What did your mom say?" Danny asked.

Will looked hard at him. Danny knew that if he hadn't been another Skin, a brother Indian, Will might have hit him for asking that.

"She doesn't know about it. She doesn't have time to know about it."

Danny looked down at Will's sneakers. He felt sad and didn't know what to say. Will reached out and pulled Danny's sleeve.

"Come on, Danno. Let's look at the exhibit. There's one that has a TV set in it and a whole bunch of things like windowpanes in front of it so that the picture reflects on all of them. You got to see the colors! It's the kind of stuff I'm going to do when I'm an artist."

Danny didn't move. Will put his right hand on Danny's shoulder.

"Danno," he said, "I'm no different 'cause I belong to a gang. I'm the same as I always was with you. You're my Indian brother." Will looked as sad as Danny felt.

Danny finally took hold of Will's elbow so that their arms were linked together.

"Okay," Danny said. He didn't know what else to say. But he knew it wasn't really okay.

▸ 7 ◂

A Falling Eagle

It wasn't a good dream. Danny sat up in bed, shaking his head to clear it away. The green numbers of the clock said it was only 6:05 in the morning. The dream had left tears in his eyes. Danny felt like getting up and climbing into bed with his mother, even though he was much too old to do that.

He kept seeing the dream. In it a beautiful eagle sat on top of a pine tree, watching over the peaceful land below it. Suddenly something came spinning out of the sky toward the eagle. Danny could see that it was going to hit the eagle and knock it out of the tree. He tried to shout a

warning, but no words would come from his mouth.

He got up and looked out the window. There was dirty snow on the streets. The wind and snow had swept in the night before. It was too early in the year for snow like this, but it had come anyway. A few cars were moving slowly on the snowy street. It looked cold out there.

It was even colder than it looked. As Danny and his mother walked to church, the wind whipped at their coats. In the stories his father told him, the winter wind was an old man with long, skinny fingers. Danny shivered at the feel of those cold fingers touching his skin.

By the time church ended, the sun had come out and the wind was gone. His father would be at work now. Danny looked up at the tops of the tallest buildings. He imagined men working up there, guiding the steel girders into place and connecting them together. They would use long-handled spud wrenches, like his father's, to turn the big steel bolts.

By late afternoon the wind had come back again. The sun was hidden behind a dark cloud and more snow was falling. Danny watched out the window, wondering what the weather was like near Philadelphia. On the map in his classroom it was farther south than New York City. Maybe it was warmer there. It probably wasn't snowing. Danny thought again about his dream and then pushed it out of his mind.

The phone rang and Danny jumped. He ran into the other room but his mother had already taken it off the wall.

"Yes, this is Salli Bigtree."

Danny stopped in front of his mother. Someone was talking on the other end. The voice sounded like the buzzing of a fly. His mother's forehead was creased with worry lines as she listened, and her eyes were shut.

"What happened?" his mother said. The fly buzzed again at the other end of the line. "I don't care about that, is he all right?" His mother turned her back to Danny and leaned her head against the wall.

Again the fly buzzed as Danny tried to understand what was being said. He knew what the call was about. He felt like a fist had been shoved into his stomach. His mother hung up the phone. She turned back to him.

"There's been an accident," she said. "Your father was hurt and we're going to him. Now." She paused. "I'll pack some clothes and your toothbrush for you. You get your coat."

Danny held his mother's hand as they sat in the subway car. He kept on holding it as they climbed onto the bus at the Port Authority Terminal. The rumble of the wheels under their seat was comforting to Danny. It reminded him of the trip they'd made a month ago up north to go back home to the rez and visit his grandparents on Cornwall Island in the middle of the St. Lawrence River.

As they sat in the bus, neither of them said much. Every ironworker's family knew that accidents could happen. But Danny had never believed his father could get hurt. He still couldn't believe it.

"He'll be okay. Right, Mom?"

"That's right, Danny," his mother said. But he could hear the worry in her voice.

His mother had thrown some food for them into a paper bag. An orange, two apples, some packages of crackers with cheese on them, a box of Oreo cookies. Every half hour they would eat something. By the time the bag was empty, it was late. Danny leaned his head against his mother's shoulder. He didn't want to fall asleep. He was afraid he would dream again. But he was very tired and so he closed his eyes. When he opened them again, there were lights all around the bus and it was slowing down.

"Philadelphia," his mother said to him.

The wind was blowing in Philadelphia too, but there was no snow on the ground. They caught a taxi outside the bus terminal. Danny was still tired and his eyes kept closing as he sat in the taxi. It didn't seem to take them long to reach the hospital.

There was a man in coveralls sitting in a chair outside the door of the hospital room they were told to go to. He didn't look Indian, though Danny knew you couldn't ever be sure. Some Mohawks had blue eyes and blond hair.

He stood up. "Hi, Mrs. Bigtree," he said. "Hal Weisser. We met before. I'm Rick's pusher."

Danny's mother nodded and Danny nodded too. He knew that the pusher was the foreman, the man with the blueprints. He and his mother were ready to go into the room and see Danny's father, but this man wanted to talk.

He needs to talk, Danny thought.

"He's okay, you know," Hal Weisser said. "What he did was he saved a man's life. It was because of the crane operator. Nobody knew he'd been drinking. I signaled him to raise the load."

Hal Weisser pointed his finger toward the ceiling and made a circle with it. Danny knew that signal. His father had taught him all the different hand signals that were used on the job.

"But instead, what he did was lower the girder. It hit the column and it spun. It woulda knocked Elbert Hill right off if your husband hadn't jumped over, just like a cat, onto the girder Elbert was on to pull him back. That spinning girder just grazed Rick, but it was enough to break his leg and knock him off the tower."

Hal Weisser was talking louder and moving his hands as he talked.

"Never saw nothing like it before. I was watching from twelve stories down." He looked at Danny, as if seeing him for the first time. "Your father?"

Danny nodded.

"Your father, I thought he was a goner. But he spread his arms out like they was wings and grabbed the beam ten foot below him as he was falling. That's when he broke his ribs. But he still hung on there until the men on the bolting crew could grab his belt and pull him in."

Hal Weisser paused. "He's mad at me 'cause I called you. Did I do the wrong thing?"

Danny's mother took Hal Weisser by the hand and then kissed him on the cheek. "You did the right thing," she said.

Hal Weisser's face got as red as a stoplight. "He was awake the last time I looked in. Now you're here, I guess I'll go back to the motel."

Richard Bigtree's face was pale. The white sheets and the hospital gown made it look paler still. He opened his eyes as they came in and he smiled. He looked better when he smiled.

"I didn't want them to tell you right away," he said. "I didn't want you to worry. It's just a busted leg and three cracked ribs."

"We're not worried," Danny's mother said. "We're here." She leaned over and kissed Danny's father and hugged him.

"Now I got four cracked ribs," Danny's father said. All three of them laughed.

While Danny's mother went to get coffee for them from the machine down the hall, Danny sat with his father.

"Dad," he said, "I had a dream last night. I saw something fall from the sky and knock an eagle out of a tree. It was scary."

Danny's father was silent for what seemed to be a long time. Then he nodded and reached his hand out to place it on Danny's chest.

"Danny," he said, "dreams are important things. You should always listen to them. But don't let them scare you. Okay?"

"Okay, Dad."

"Looks like I'll be home for a while. Maybe I'll put that degree I got from Potsdam College to work and do some substitute teaching. Doesn't pay like ironwork does, but you don't get your ribs broke when you fall off a desk."

Danny laughed, but it was a short laugh. His father's joke had made him remember school.

Danny's father looked closely at him. "What happened to your nose and your lip?"

"Basketball."

"I didn't know you played."

"I don't. Tyrone hit me in the face with his basketball." Danny hadn't meant to cry, but there were tears in his eyes now.

Danny's father nodded. "Things didn't get better right away after I visited the school, eh?"

"No."

"It's hard to believe in peace, Danny. There's a lot of danger in the world. Things happen when you don't expect them. There's so many people who will tell you that it doesn't make any sense to believe in peace. But it takes a lot more courage to make a friend sometimes than it does to make an enemy. Having friends is a risky thing, you might say."

"Elbert Hill is your friend, isn't he?"

Danny's father chuckled. "You could say that. He's gotten me in trouble more than once, though. I ever tell you how we tipped over his grandmother's outhouse when we were kids? When his grandmother asked at dinner about who did it, we confessed. His grandmother had told us about how when George Washington was a little boy he cut down his father's cherry tree. And when George confessed, he didn't get punished because he told the truth. You know that story, don't you?"

Danny nodded.

Danny's father chuckled again and pressed his hand to his side.

"Got to remember not to laugh with these cracked ribs. So when Elbert and I confessed, we figured we would be home free. But Elbert's grandmother grabbed him and started swatting him on the butt with her cane. Elbert hollered out, 'When George Washington confessed that he cut down his father's cherry tree, his father didn't whomp him.' And Elbert's grandma, she hollered, 'George Washington's father was not in that cherry tree when it got cut down!' "

Danny shook his head and then began to laugh. Cracked ribs and all, his father laughed with him. Everything was going to be okay after all.

▸ 8 ◂
Peace

Danny missed school on Monday. They spent the day bringing his father back home. He wasn't hurt so badly that he needed to stay in the hospital.

"I'd rather save my health insurance for sometime when I really need it," he said.

On Tuesday Danny's father wrote the note for Danny to take to school to explain his absence. As Danny started out the door, his father called out to him.

"Danny?"

"Yeah, Dad?"

"She':kon."

"She':kon, Dad."

Danny arrived at school early enough so the morning bell had not yet rung. Lots of kids were still outside. Tyrone and Brad were there by the steps, tossing their basketball back and forth between them.

Danny took a deep breath and walked toward them. He stopped when he was six feet from the boys.

"Yo!" Brad said. He backed away.

Tyrone stared at Danny, but Danny didn't move.

"You want to fight me, man?" Tyrone said.

Danny shook his head. "Not unless I have to."

"Are you okay?" Tyrone said. "I didn't mean to hit you so hard with the ball."

"I'm okay."

Tyrone smiled. "Anyhow, Hiawatha, you cool. You didn't tell on me."

Danny didn't smile back. "My name isn't Hiawatha. And it isn't Chief. My name is Daniel."

Tyrone laughed. "Okay, Daniel. So what you want?"

"I just don't want us to be enemies," Danny said. "Maybe we could be friends." He held out his hand. *"She':kon?* That means 'peace.'"

Tyrone took his hand.

"We're not enemies," Tyrone said. *"She':kon,* man."

Then the bell rang, calling them into school.

That night, just before he went to bed, Danny walked over to look out his window again. It was hard to see much in the dark, but the snow on the streets didn't look as dirty. He looked out from the window for a long time. He thought of all the people going by in the cars below, about the people behind the other lighted windows of this city and the other cities, people who needed to hear a hymn of peace. He thought about Will Tiger and the other kids who felt they had to join gangs to belong.

He knew that he wanted to be like Aionwahta. He wanted to be like his father. He wanted to always hold that song of peace in his heart. He would talk to Will about the idea of peace when they were together again. Maybe Will would be ready to listen.

Glossary ▸ Pronunciation Guide

Adodarhonh (Ah-to-TAR-ho): Leader of the Onondagas, literally "Tangled," referring to the snakes tangled in his hair.

Aionwahta (Ay-yon-WAH-tah): One of the two founders of the Iroquois league, literally "He Who Combs."

Akwesasne (Ah-kway-SAH-snee): Mohawk Nation reservation located on the U.S.–Canadian border, along the St. Lawrence River; literally "The Place Where the Partridge Drums."

Gustoweh (KUS-to-wey): A traditional Mohawk cap.

Henh (heynh): Mohawk word for yes.

She':kon (SAY-goh): Mohawk word of greeting, meaning "peace."

Yah-tah-hey (YAH-tah-hey): Navajo word for hello.